DISNEY

GiRL
meets
WORLD

FRIEND POWER

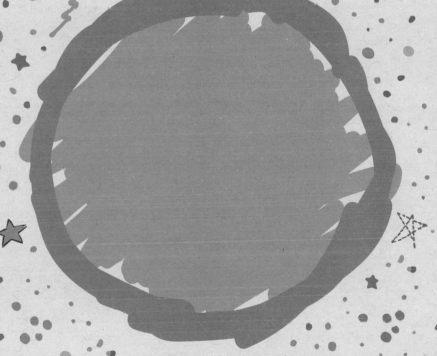

Adapted by Alexa Young
Based on the series created by Michael Jacobs and April Kelly
Part One is based on the episode "Girl Meets the Tell-Tale Tot," written by Teresa Kale.
Part Two is based on the episode "Girl Meets the New World," written by Teresa Kale.

DISNEY PRESS
Los Angeles · New York

SUSTAINABLE
FORESTRY
INITIATIVE

Certified Chain of Custody
Promoting Sustainable Forestry

www.sfiprogram.org
SFI-01054

The SFI label applies to the text stock

PART ONE

CHAPTER 1

It was a typical morning at the Matthews apartment. Riley sat on her usual bench at the breakfast table with her dad to her right and her mom and little brother, Auggie, seated across from her. The eggs, toast, and fruit were standard before-school fare. The only thing *not* typical? Riley's best friend, Maya Hart, wasn't there with them. Yet.

"All right, weirdos, listen up and listen up good!" Maya declared as she rolled in like a tornado and zoomed through the living room. "I only got like a minute before he walks through that door!"

"Who's coming through the door, Maya?" Riley spun around on the bench and smiled.

"Your uncle Boing," Maya replied.

"Oh, Maya, you gotta get offa this!" Riley reached out to give her friend's shoulder a concerned squeeze. Ever since poor Maya had met him, she'd had a serious thing for Riley's uncle Josh—her dad's much younger brother—hence Maya's nickname for him: Uncle Boing.

"Nope," Maya insisted, pacing around the apartment as she shared a new theory about her tragically one-sided crush. "The reason he's not interested is because I've been playin' it wrong. See, my strategy of turning into a total nut job at the mere sight of him ain't working out as planned."

Riley shook her head, amazed that her best friend, who was normally so wise when it came to pretty much everything in life, could be so clueless about this. "Maya, it's nothing you're doing. It's the age difference."

"Three years older!" Maya scrunched up her face, not buying Riley's interpretation. "Your dad married your mom and he's like twenty years older!"

Hmmm. She did have a point.

"We're *exactly* the same age!" Riley's dad, Cory, interjected.

"What?" Riley spun back around on the bench and shot a bewildered glare at her father. Her parents stared back at her in amazement, as if she should have realized this. Well, okay, she knew they were *about* the same age. But her dad had a different kind of vibe from her mom. An *old person* vibe.

"I just need to be cazh." Maya returned the conversation to her previous line of reasoning as she sat down next to Riley. She swung her chunky black suede boots up onto the table and leaned against her friend awkwardly, tossing back her long blond hair and striking a pose that was anything *but* casual. "How's this?"

Riley's mom, Topanga, immediately got up and marched over, then pushed Maya's feet away from the food. "Yeah, how's *this*?"

Just then, Uncle Josh walked through the door, looking extremely mature in a bright blue button-down shirt and black vest. "Hey, family," he said with a broad, dimpled smile.

"Yeah, hi, I don't care," Maya muttered under her breath, rolling her eyes and twirling a piece of hair around her finger.

"My *brother*!" Josh called out to Riley's dad as he tossed his bag on the couch and walked to the breakfast table.

"*My* brother!" Riley's dad called back. He was excited Josh had come to visit.

"So, Riley," Maya said while inspecting her nails, continuing to focus her attention on *anything* but Josh, "shouldn't we be, like, heading to school now, since there's nothing here for me of any interest?"

Ha. Okay, fine. Riley was more than happy to play along with her best friend's plan. "Sure, let's go," she agreed.

"Think she'll make it out the door?" Auggie whispered to his big sister, proving that Maya's calm, cool, and collected act wasn't fooling even the youngest person in the room.

Riley leaned across the table and looked into her little brother's eyes with a sly smile. "I give her ten seconds before she jumps on his head!" she predicted, then got up and followed Maya to the door.

"I came up here because I wanted to do this in front of all of you," Josh announced. "I hold in my hand an envelope from New York University."

When she heard those words, Maya stopped so suddenly that Riley bumped right into her back. "Oh, are we stopping?" Riley practically sang with a giant knowing grin as she looked from Maya to Josh and back to Maya.

"I'm not stopping, I'm *resting*," Maya insisted, feet firmly planted until Riley gave her a gentle nudge forward.

"What's in this envelope tells me where I'm going to be for the next four years," Josh continued, prompting Maya to stop—and Riley to bump into her—again.

"Oh, are we stopping?" Riley repeated, choking down a laugh. Maya was being about as casual as a prom dress.

"I'm not as young as I used to be," Maya explained feebly before continuing to trudge to the door.

"Good luck, Josh!" Riley called out.

"Yeah, hi, I don't care," Maya added as they finally exited the apartment.

As if under a spell, Josh stared after the girls and took a few steps toward the closed door. "Is it just me or is there a new maturity in Maya that I haven't seen before?" he murmured. "I find it intriguing."

Suddenly, the door swung open and a wild-eyed Maya, no longer able to contain herself, screamed, "Where will you beeeeee?" She ran to Josh and jumped onto his back, grabbing for the envelope in his hand and nearly knocking him down as he spun and staggered around the room, desperately trying to get her off him.

"Hold on to your dignity, woman!" Riley shouted.

"Too late for that," Auggie pointed out as Josh continued to flail around.

"Get offa me, ya little ferret!" Josh kept spinning in a desperate attempt to free himself from Maya, who was still trying to snatch the envelope from his clutches.

"Give it!" Maya screamed, finally getting hold of her target.

"It's *my* life!" Josh yelled back.

"Well, it affects me, too!" Maya insisted, tearing open the large manila envelope and beginning to read the letter while still seated on Josh's back like a rodeo star. "Dear Applicant Boing—"

"It doesn't *say* that!" Josh shouted, trying once again to shake Maya loose.

"This year we are only accepting married applicants—" Maya continued.

"It doesn't *say* that!" Josh repeated, louder.

"Therefore, we regret to inform you—"

"Regret to inform me?" Josh's face fell and he finally stopped trying to eject Maya, who continued to read in a softer voice.

"We regret to inform you that you will be spending the next four years . . ." Maya paused briefly and then blurted out excitedly, "IN NEW YORK WITH MAYYYYYAAAAAA!"

"I got in?" Josh asked in amazement as Maya slid down to the floor. "I got in!" Josh's face lit up like a Christmas tree as he spun around to beam at Maya.

"We got in! Congratulations, Josh!" Maya gushed, opening her arms to give him a hug.

But before they could connect, the whole family swept Josh into a group hug and Maya fell backward onto the couch.

"Yayyy!" shouted Riley.

"Way to go!" Mrs. Matthews joined in.

"You did it!" Mr. Matthews bellowed.

"I don't know what this means!" Auggie added in his adorably oblivious way.

"Congratulations, buddy," Mr. Matthews said, wrapping an arm around Josh. "I'm so proud of you!"

"That means a lot to me, Cory," Josh replied.

As she observed the family celebration, Maya switched back into casual mode. "All very exciting,

I'm sure, but Riley and I have our own educations to which to attend . . . to which . . ." Maya's voice trailed off as she took Riley's hand and led her toward the door.

"This is so great," Josh raved to Mr. Matthews. "And my buddy who goes there invited me to his dorm tonight to meet some college friends if I got in."

At the front door, Maya paused and Riley bumped into her. Again.

"Oh, are we stopping?" Riley cooed, as entertained as she had been the past two times.

"Nope, we're doing something else now," Maya replied slyly, pulling Riley back into the apartment. As they breezed past Josh, she ever-so-nonchalantly inquired, "When is this little party, yeah, whatever, hi, I don't care?"

"Ten o'clock tonight," Josh told her.

"And where is this little party, yeah, whatever, hi, I don't care?" Maya asked.

"Greenwich Hall," Josh replied.

A victorious grin spread across Maya's face.

"Are we smiling?" Riley beamed back at her best friend. "I'll smile. I'll smile anytime. What are we smiling about?"

"Bay window. Bay window right now!" Maya linked arms with Riley and hauled her upstairs to Riley's bedroom. "Can I sleep over at your house tonight?" she asked when they were safely inside.

"Yay!" Riley agreed, always happy to have a slumber party with her best friend in the whole wide world.

"But not really," Maya continued.

"Aww." Riley frowned.

"I'm going to that party," Maya announced.

"Ooooh, you're going to sneak out?" Riley bounced up and down in her chunky black boots until her memory of the specifics brought her back down to earth. "But he said it could go till ten o'clock!"

"No, it starts at ten," Maya said, correcting her, as she walked to the window seat.

"It *starts* at ten?" Riley shuddered at the absurdity

of a party—or anything—starting so late at night. "Who even heard of such a thing?"

"That bothers you, huh?" Maya smirked.

"It *starts* at ten?" Riley flung up her arms and marched over to sit next to Maya on the comfy purple cushions.

"There are going to be college girls there," Maya explained carefully. "And they're pretty. And they're smart. And they're *witches*."

Riley shook her head, growing more disturbed by the second as she raised a single eyebrow. "I don't like witches."

"We can't let Josh fall under their spell, Riley," Maya insisted. "I'm sneaking out."

Riley couldn't allow it. "You will be grounded forever and I will lose my best friend," she cautioned Maya. "Don't do this!"

But Maya wasn't budging. "No. I am not gonna look back and regret the things I didn't do. I wanna look back and regret the things I . . . *did* do!" Even Maya didn't seem entirely convinced by the last bit.

"You can't do this," Riley said. "Your conscience will always bother you."

"I don't have a conscience."

"Everyone does," Riley argued, but she could see from the blank look on Maya's face that her best friend wasn't buying it. So she quickly switched gears. "And until yours shows up, I'm going with you."

"Oh, really?" Maya said. "You're ready to sneak out the window and crash a ten o'clock college party with me?"

"I am so ready!" Riley insisted, desperately trying to convince herself as much as anyone else. But she needed to clarify something, for the record, one last time. "It *starts* at ten?"

Maya nodded.

Ugh. There were so many things wrong with the plan. It wasn't just about when the party would start but about where—and how—everything would end. But that was precisely why Riley couldn't let Maya go alone.

CHAPTER 2

Later that morning, Riley was finding it impossible to concentrate on the day's history lesson. Her mind was too focused on the future as she played out all the possible ways things could go down if Maya really snuck out that night.

"Okay, how are we pulling this caper off?" Riley loud-whispered to Maya.

But her best friend was still adamant about going alone. "Riley, if we snuck out for an adventure, I know you'd tell your parents," she said with a sigh.

"I promise I won't!" Riley insisted.

Mr. Matthews looked up from his desk. "Who's talking?" he barked at the class.

Ever the dutiful daughter and student, Riley immediately and instinctively raised her hand. "We are, it's us!"

Oops. Riley cringed, realizing she'd done exactly what Maya had predicted.

"You ain't going," Maya concluded as Mr. Matthews continued with his lecture.

"What is a lie?" he asked, standing in front of the chalkboard, where the word *conscience* was written in big, bold letters. "What are the effects of a lie on the human soul?"

Ohmygosh. Did he already know what Riley and Maya were planning to do that night? Could Riley's dad see everything that was going on inside her head without her even telling him? How did he *do* that?

"Why are you looking at *me*?" Riley demanded, widening her eyes innocently in the hopes that her dad would move on—which, fortunately, he did.

"The man who summed up the price of a lie was Edgar Allan Poe in *The Tell-Tale Heart*," Mr.

Matthews said, holding up a copy of the book and then gesturing to Farkle to take over the lesson.

But before Farkle could say anything, Isaiah "Zay" Babineaux began speaking with a dramatic intensity. "So, this guy chops somebody up, hides him in the floor. He's cool for a while but all of a sudden"— Zay was delighting in every gruesome detail as he opened and closed his hand like a beating heart— "boom boom . . . boom boom . . . boom BOOM!" Zay smacked his hand down on his desk so hard that everyone nearly jumped out of their seats. "His guilty conscience made him hear the heart beat under the floorboards. So he gave himself up. Some people just aren't cut out for this stuff."

Farkle was not happy that Zay had stolen the spotlight. "He called on *me*, y'know."

"I know stuff! I know a *lot* of stuff," Zay fired back, then walked over to stare Farkle down as he added in a sinister voice, "I know stuff about *you*."

"You don't know anything about me," Farkle insisted quickly, his eyes darting away from Zay.

"Boom boom," Zay repeated, once again opening and closing his hand like a beating heart as he pushed it closer and closer to Farkle's face.

"Why would you do that?" Farkle's voice trembled and he shifted uncomfortably in his seat.

"Boom boom," Zay continued, louder.

"I don't understand why you would do that!" Farkle's voice was pleading.

"Boom *BOOM!*" Zay nearly shouted.

That was it. Farkle couldn't take it anymore. He broke down and confessed to what he apparently thought Zay was trying to get out of him. "All through kindergarten I never fell asleep once!" Farkle sputtered. "I was faking all of my naps! Faking 'em! I can't do it! I don't know how Maya can just fall asleep anywhere!"

At that revelation, Mr. Matthews began to examine Maya, his jaw dropping in awe as he realized that although her eyes were wide open, the girl was fast asleep, judging from the buzz saw–like noises she was making.

Undeterred, Mr. Matthews carried on with his

lesson. "Okay, so, guys, the point of the story is that the conscience is more powerful than we realize—" He suddenly paused and slammed his book down on Maya's desk.

"I never wake *you* up!" Maya shouted as she bolted awake.

"—for those of us who have one," Mr. Matthews continued with a smirk. "Now, just as the truth comes out, so, too, will a lie. How will you live your lives? How strong is your conscience?"

Oh, no. No, no, no! Riley's face crumpled and her palms grew sweaty as her heart—her poor little telltale heart—beat in double time, echoing in her head with a haunting *boom boom*. Her father was definitely on to her and Maya! He knew everything about their plan to sneak out that night. They were doomed. *Doomed!*

Maya, observing the freaked-out expression on Riley's face, narrowed her eyes and informed her friend, "We haven't done anything yet."

"Oh, yeah!" Riley breathed a sigh of relief. Her face broke into a giant smile and she began swaying to the magical, innocent sound of happy elf music that played in her head when all was right with the world. Everything was still okay. Riley was content to be in her happy place and move to her internal music knowing she hadn't done anything wrong . . . at least not yet.

CHAPTER 3

As Riley's mom served a dinner of chicken, veggies, and potato tots that evening, Riley turned to look at Maya. Riley knew that with the right approach, she could get her friend to see that having her at the party would be the best thing for both of them.

"Before you give up on me completely, you gotta give me a trial run at least," Riley proposed, grabbing Maya's arm intently. "You gotta, Maya. You just gotta."

Maya's eyes bulged out and she began to make a groaning noise, kind of like her head was a balloon and Riley was slowly making the air escape from it. Riley knew that sound all too well. It was the sound of victory, the sound of her finally wearing Maya down!

"Yayyy!" Riley grinned. "If I succeed?"

"I take you," Maya grumbled. "And if you fail?"

"I'm out. I'm out like a light," Riley swore, even though failure was not an option.

"Okay." Maya nodded wearily and looked at Mr. Matthews, who was pointing at his plate and counting. "What's he doin'?"

"He loves his tots," Riley whispered.

"Eight, nine, ten." Mr. Matthews's face clouded over with confusion. "Ten tots. Auggie, how many you got?"

"Twelve!" Auggie declared, holding one up like a tiny trophy.

"Gimme." Mr. Matthews reached out for the golden morsel.

"Do I have to?" Auggie complained, hesitating before finally agreeing to pass it down the table to his father.

Riley knew the whole thing must have looked weird to an outside observer, but it had been a completely normal part of the potato tot dining experience for as long as she could remember. "He counts the tots on everybody's plate to make sure nobody gets more than him," she explained to Maya.

"That's not what I do!" Mr. Matthews insisted, then launched into a lecture that made sense to nobody but him. "I know one thing for sure about life. Ten tots are one tot too little, and twelve tots are one tot too much."

Maya elbowed her best friend. "Watch this, Riley," she whispered before turning to Riley's dad. "Mr. Matthews, you're lookin' good. Are you wearing your hair different?"

Mrs. Matthews wrinkled her nose as she looked at her husband. "How would that be possible?"

"Thank you, Maya." Mr. Matthews beamed with pride, ignoring his wife's question and laughing with a hint of false modesty as he pretended to pat down his dark curls without actually touching them. "Lotta work. This doesn't just happen."

As Mr. Matthews spoke, Maya's hand darted over and snagged a tot from his plate, then swiftly plunked it down in front of Riley. Nobody at the table seemed to notice the crime that had occurred—nobody, that is, except Riley, whose eyes grew wide with horror as she stared down at the pilfered potato. The longer Riley stared at it, the more the tot seemed to take on a life of its own. Then she would have sworn she could hear the sound of creepy organ music playing as the tot appeared to sprout a pair of eyes!

"What's the matter with Riley?" Auggie asked when he heard his sister gasp and caught the look of terror on her face.

"I don't know, Auggie," Maya replied innocently, turning to look at her friend. "Riley, is there something wrong?"

"Yuh-huh." Riley nodded dizzily while staring at the tater face.

Suddenly, the tot grew, until it was almost as big as Riley's head! Her guilty conscience had taken on the form of a giant talking potato tot. Sure, it was crazy, but it seemed very real to Riley.

"Boom boom," the giant tot jeered, echoing the sound of her frantic heartbeat.

Riley recoiled in fear, nearly falling backward off the bench. "You know what? I'm not really hungry," she announced, motioning to the freakish food on her plate. "Does anybody else want this?"

"No, Riley. It's yours. Eat it," Maya said tersely, then lowered her voice to a growl and repeated with a menacing grin, "Eaaat iiiit." To her, it just looked like a normal tot.

Riley couldn't possibly eat that . . . that . . . *thing*! But she knew she had to. This was her trial run. She had to pass the test!

"What happens if I eat you?" Riley whispered so only the giant tot could hear her.

"Oh. I become part of your soul and haunt you forever . . . *ever* . . . *ever.* . . ." The scary spud's words echoed loudly in Riley's ears as it quickly, and kindly, added, "Enjoy me. They tell me I'm delicious!"

Riley's stomach was in knots. This wasn't going well at all.

"Riley, are you going to eat this, or are you not going?" Maya demanded.

"I'm going!" Riley insisted as Maya picked up the tot—which had miraculously returned to its former size—and shoved it into Riley's mouth.

"Swallow it," Maya commanded, holding Riley's head to make sure the whole thing went down.

But as soon as the tot began its descent, Riley was certain she heard it calling out to her: "Here I go. Wheeeee!"

Well, at least the tot sounded happy about the situation. That had to count for something, didn't it? Maybe it was just a matter of Riley's controlling her conscience rather than her conscience's controlling her!

CHAPTER 4

Although her stomach wasn't feeling completely settled, Riley was proud of herself for triumphing in the potato tot trial run. The taste of victory was so sweet that it almost completely masked the guilt she expected to feel. Sitting there next to Maya in the bay window of her bedroom, she was certain she could pass the next test, too.

"So I'm in, right?" Riley asked eagerly.

"Yes," Maya grumbled.

"Squeee!" Riley cheered.

"All right, first thing we're gonna need is another Riley." Maya jumped up and marched to Riley's bed.

"Why?" Riley asked.

"Your parents are going to open the door to check on you, and it needs to look like you're in here," Maya explained as she pulled back the comforter and arranged the big purple pillows in a line before covering them back up.

Seriously? That was Maya's master plan for getting away with the major stunt they were about to attempt?

"Maya! How could it possibly happen where anyone would ever believe that was actually me under the covers? I mean, who would be dumb enough to fall for—" Riley stopped short, stunned by what Maya had just done. There was definitely somebody in Riley's bed now. It was incredible. So lifelike. It really *was* another Riley! "How did I get over there?"

Maya shrugged with a self-congratulatory grin. "'Cause I'm the best there is at what I do."

Riley stepped a bit closer to the bed, still marveling at Maya's convincing work. "Night night, fake Riley," she said softly to the line of pillows. "I was once as innocent as you. But now all I have to do is climb out that window and then I am just like this wicked woman over here." Riley flung an arm around Maya's shoulders and gave her a giant guilt-free hug.

"Riley, if you just let it happen, there's a chance we can actually get away with this," Maya informed her.

"Right. Sure. I'm letting it happen." Riley rubbed her hands together, feeling more confident with each passing second. "First time I ever tried something like this and I am going to get away with it. Y'know why? Because I, like you, have no conscience!"

"Great. Let's go." Maya turned away from Riley and headed out the window.

But before Riley could follow, the giant tot was back. It was sitting right there on the window ledge, staring at her with those creepy eyes!

"Boom boom," declared the tot, sounding less like a heart beating and more like a heart . . . *bleating*.

This time, however, it was gone almost as quickly as it had appeared. Was it possible that Riley's conscience had disappeared with it? Could she really be exactly like Maya?

"Okay. This is going to be an interesting night," Riley noted as she switched off the light and climbed out the window. It was time for the real test—no more trial runs—and she was determined to pass.

CHAPTER 5

Before she knew it, Riley was following Maya through the halls of a giant building at NYU. *New York University!* She felt so tiny—like Alice in Wonderland after swallowing the "Drink Me" potion—as she looked at all the *big* college students milling around in their *big* clothes with their *big* backpacks and *big* lives. She became positively dizzy as she and Maya wandered past the walls plastered with flyers advertising lectures and tutoring and parties and fund-raisers.

"I can't believe I snuck out the window," Riley marveled. "I've never been to a college. They're gonna know I don't belong here."

"Don't talk," Maya scolded her. "Just act like you fit in."

Riley pressed her lips together, eager to obey Maya's orders. But telling Riley not to talk was like telling her not to breathe. "I wanna talk so bad!" she finally blurted out.

"You don't know what to say," Maya reminded her. "You've never been to a college before."

Oh. Right. Riley nodded and tried to focus on the letters of a poster but impulsively shouted out, "Beat Notre Dame!"

"Yeeeeaaaahhhh!" roared a group of giant guys in NYU sweatshirts and jackets as they rushed over and hoisted Riley onto their shoulders. Then they whooped and carried her down the hall like a championship trophy.

For a fleeting moment, Riley felt like she actually did fit in! But that sense of belonging promptly turned into a sense of terror. "Mayyyaaaaa!" she screamed.

"Give her back," Maya called after them.

Fortunately, the NYU jocks were good listeners.

They turned right around and set Riley down in the same spot where they'd found her, then cheered and hollered as they raced out of the building.

"See you at the game, boys!" Riley shouted, beaming with pride and waving a newly acquired NYU pennant.

"Riley—" Maya sighed.

"If you talk here, they pick you up and they carry you!" Riley exclaimed, noticing a sudden shift taking place, almost like she and Maya were swapping identities.

"That's ridiculous," Maya replied sensibly.

"Oh, yeah?" Riley knew what she was talking about. She knew exactly how this whole college thing worked now. Because she was letting it happen. To prove it to Maya, she looked at another sign stuck to a bulletin board and proclaimed, "Gamma Gamma Nu!"

A group of girls in bright pink tees and sweatshirts emblazoned with Greek letters raced over, then squealed as they picked up Riley and carried her off.

"Give her back," Maya called after them wearily. The sorority girls were good listeners, too.

"I just pledged!" Riley told Maya, tugging at the collar of her bright yellow sweater to show her friend the shiny star-shaped pin she'd just received. "I don't want to wait for college to be real. I'm staying!"

Maya rolled her eyes and stared down the hall but then quickly looked back at Riley. "We're leaving," she said softly.

"Why?" Riley asked. How could Maya want to leave? College was the most magical place ever!

"I got here too late," Maya explained, glancing back down the hall, where laughter could be heard coming from an open doorway.

Right inside the door, Riley saw her uncle Josh sitting on a bed next to a girl with rosy cheeks and long, wavy brown hair. She wore a red hooded sweater. Straining to hear their conversation, Riley could just make out what Josh was saying.

"So, how long did it take for you guys to feel comfortable here?" he asked the girl.

"It's about the people you meet, really," she replied with a confident smile.

Josh smiled back and extended his hand. "It's nice to meet you."

"You too." The girl grinned, taking his hand and shaking it.

Out in the hall, Riley could practically hear Maya's heart breaking.

"How did I think I could ever compete with them?" Maya frowned.

But Riley knew exactly what to do. "Maya, a Gamma Gamma girl does not let her sister give up at the first sign of trouble."

"You're not a Gamma Gamma girl!" Maya fired back as a perky brunette in a tight pink shirt and an extremely short miniskirt rushed over.

"Ri-Ri, you totally ditched us!" The girl pouted.

"I'm dealing with some stuff, Harriet," Riley replied firmly.

The girl was undeterred. Her whole face lit up as she looked at Riley and said, "I shouldn't tell you this, but you were already voted best friend to have."

What?! Riley could hardly believe her ears. "I thought Gretchen had that!"

"Nope! You!" Harriet pointed at Riley and then flung open her arms. "Gamma song?"

"Of course Gamma song!" Riley agreed—and with that, she and Harriet launched into the routine her new sisters had been amazed to see her pick up so quickly, singing:

We are the sisters of Gamma Gamma Nu.
We are humble but we're better than you.
We help people everywhere
But we still love our hair, 'cause we're Gamma
*   Gamma Nu!*

Then, for the grand finale—Riley's favorite part—she and Harriet both flipped their hair, extended their arms, and insisted, with exaggerated humility, "Stop it!"

"That's *ours!*" Maya yelled when she saw the familiar hair-flip-stop-it move.

"Grow up," Riley shot back without skipping a beat. This whole take-charge, girl-in-control thing was kind of exhilarating.

"I'm leaving." Maya scowled and tried to dart away.

"You're not." Riley grabbed Maya's shoulders in an attempt to both stop her and shake some sense into her.

"Riley, how do I even begin to compete with those girls in there?" Maya whimpered, motioning to the dorm room where Josh was hanging out with his new friends.

Inside, Riley could hear another guy saying, "See, Josh? Nothing to worry about at all. You're gonna fit right in here."

"Yeah, you've got new friends already, and a new life waiting as soon as you get here," agreed the rosy-cheeked girl.

Each happy word they said about Josh's future

life with them seemed to send a tiny dagger into Maya's heart. "Yeah, he's gone," she told Riley. "Please take me home."

But Riley wasn't going to let her best friend give up that easily. "Bold women make bold choices," she insisted.

Maya shook her head at Riley, her blue eyes tearing up. "What does that even mean?"

"It's a Gamma thing," Riley explained. "It's what we say right before we shove a sister into a bold choice."

With that, Riley grabbed Maya by the shoulders again, spun her around, and pushed her directly into the dorm room. Even the look of utter shock that flashed across Josh's face couldn't discourage Riley. Not only was she letting things happen and getting away with it, as Maya had advised her; she was *making* things happen and getting away with it. So long, conscience—hello, college!

CHAPTER 6

Back at the Matthews apartment, Auggie couldn't fall asleep—and anytime that happened, all he wanted to do was snuggle up in bed with his big sister.

"Riley," he whispered, tiptoeing into her bedroom and softly closing the door behind him. "Can I sleep with you tonight?"

Auggie continued to creep to the bed. "You're not saying no?" he whispered with hopeful glee. "Does that mean yes?"

Finally, he climbed up and smiled at the figure in the bed. "Good night."

Reaching over to give Riley a hug, Auggie

immediately sensed that something was very, very wrong. That wasn't Riley! She was too soft. Too fluffy. He pounced on the figure in the bed and pulled back the covers to discover nothing but a giant line of pillows.

"Uh-oh, Riley's being a bad girl," he said, clucking, as someone knocked on the door.

Auggie put the covers back over fake Riley just in time.

"Auggie, what are you doing in here?" asked Mrs. Matthews when she saw her little boy, still awake, sitting on the bed.

"I'm sleeping over at Riley's," he explained sweetly. "We love each other."

"Is that okay with Riley?" Mrs. Matthews asked, leaning into the room and looking at the figure in the bed. "Riley?"

"Shhh, Mommy," Auggie whispered, holding a finger up to his lips. "She's really sleepy."

Mrs. Matthews smiled proudly at her son. "Aren't you just the best little brother?"

"You have no idea," Auggie replied with a wide Cheshire cat grin. "G'night."

"Good night," Mrs. Matthews replied, waving to her little boy and gently closing the door.

With his mom safely out of earshot, Auggie turned back to look down at fake Riley. "I own you now!" he proclaimed before leaping onto the pile of pillows and rolling around giddily.

Of course, falling asleep was going to be even more impossible now. Auggie could hardly contain his excitement, thinking about all the things he might do to make his sister repay him for the secret he'd kept for her. The way he saw it, Riley's being bad was going to equal a whole lot of good—for him, anyway.

CHAPTER 7

As Riley and Maya stood in the doorway of the dorm room, Riley's eyes widened in amazement. It was kind of like her room, but even cooler—with a big round green rug on the floor, strings of little fairy lights stretching across the ceiling, and artsy posters and family photos adorning the walls.

But Josh's eyes were wide with a different kind of amazement. "Maya? Riley?" he said, getting up from the bed.

"You know these girls, Josh?" asked a big muscular guy who was on the other bed across the room. He stood up and smiled warmly at Maya and Riley. "How ya doin'?"

Before Riley could respond, Maya blurted out, "We're in middle school."

The guy leapt backward. "Ho! They can't be here, Josh!"

"No kidding," Josh agreed, taking a step toward the girls. He addressed his niece. "Riley. What are you thinking? You have to go."

But once again, Maya spoke up first. "You're right, Josh," she said solemnly. "We're sorry. This was a bad idea."

Maya grabbed Riley by the arm and tried to lead her out of the room, but before they could make it to the door, the girl with the wavy brown hair stopped them. "Wait. Intrigued." She pushed Josh out of the way so he fell back onto the bed. "Maya? What was your bad idea?"

Maya looked at the girl and tried to explain. "He's her uncle Josh. I call him Uncle Boing, because look at him."

"She made me sneak out a window to come here," Riley said, continuing the story. "That's how much she likes him. Because she was afraid that you guys were witches and you would steal him from her."

On the bed, poor Josh, who was clearly mortified, planted his face in his palms.

"They're not witches, Riley," Maya acknowledged softly. "They're girls who don't live at home anymore and know a lot more than we do."

Riley didn't want to give up that easily, but Maya seemed resigned. "Sorry we interrupted your evening," Riley said to the girls before turning back toward the door.

But this time, another girl, with straight black hair and a long purple sweater, stopped them. "Oh, I think our evening has just begun," the girl said, putting an arm around Maya's shoulders and leading her back into the room.

As Riley was about to join Maya on the bed with the other girls, Harriet and the Gamma girls rushed in through the door. "Initiation!" Harriet squealed, pulling a fuzzy pink blindfold over Riley's eyes.

"Yayyy!" Riley screamed along with her new sisters as they hurried her out the door.

"All right, bring her back," Josh called after them.

That was when Harriet noticed the other guy in the room. "Andrew?" she gasped, and scrunched up her nose. "You told me you died."

"I did, I am," Andrew replied, rising from the bed. He added in a haunting whisper, "Don't forget me." With that, he walked out into the hall.

"They all die." Harriet frowned, perplexed, as she left the room.

"Hey," the girl with the rosy cheeks and red sweater said to Maya.

"Hey," Maya replied with a nervous little wave as she settled between the two girls on the bed.

"So, Maya, what do you see in this guy?" rosy cheeks asked.

"How long have you had a crush on him?" added the girl in the purple sweater.

Maya shook her head. "It's not a crush. It isn't.

Maybe I'm not as old as you guys, but I know what I feel."

"Hey, I've never done anything like what you're doing." Purple sweater seemed impressed.

"Yeah, it makes you pretty grown-up to me," rosy cheeks agreed.

Maya searched for the right words to explain why she'd snuck out. "I just thought if I did something like this, he might take me seriously and maybe we could come to some kind of understanding."

Josh, who was walking back into the room with Andrew and Riley in tow, looked straight at Maya. "We *have* an understanding," he told her. "I stay here. You go home."

"Sit down," the girls on either side of Maya commanded Josh.

"Okay," Josh quickly agreed with a self-conscious laugh, racing over to sit on the other bed with Andrew while Riley remained in the doorway.

"I'm just stupid, right?" Maya said to nobody in particular.

Andrew shook his head sweetly at Maya. "Hey, I would love it if somebody did something stupid for me."

"Yeah," rosy cheeks agreed. "It's not the big gestures that we do for other people that help us grow up—"

"But the small choices you make for yourself," added purple sweater.

As Maya looked from one girl to the other gratefully, Riley got the distinct impression that she'd missed something big while she was off with her Gamma sisters. "Ohhh," she said as it dawned on her. "Maya told you guys about her crush."

"It's not a crush!" Maya jumped up from the bed and walked over to Riley.

"Maya." Riley stared into her best friend's bright blue eyes, which suddenly seemed so innocent. "Can you name one thing you know about him that you love?"

"He's part of your family, Riley." Maya looked intently at her friend. "And I love your family."

"And we love you." Riley saw that she was going to have to press a little harder on this one. "But what about Josh in particular?"

"Yeah," Josh agreed from the bed. "Maya, you don't even really know me."

Maya turned around and looked straight at Josh. "Yeah. You're right. I don't pay attention to anything you do," she acknowledged with a smirk. "I don't know that you would drive from Philadelphia to New York not even looking if you got into NYU just so you could open your acceptance letter in front of your older brother because you love him and you want him to be proud of you."

Okay. Score one for Maya.

Maya took a few steps toward Josh, who leaned in a little closer, his dark eyes widening with genuine surprise as Maya continued. "And I see the way you are with Auggie, a little kid who looks up to you, who you always have time for."

Point two goes to Maya!

"And I know that even though you'd rather stay

49

here with these girls, you're going to walk Riley and me home, because that's just the kind of guy you are."

Game, set, and match to Maya! Apparently, it really wasn't a crush after all. Riley knew it, Maya knew it, and—Riley could tell from looking around the room—Josh and his new friends knew it, too.

"I like you," Maya finally concluded.

"Dude." Andrew turned to look at Josh. "What is *wrong* with you?"

"She's three years younger than me!" Josh argued, standing up.

"Sit down," commanded rosy cheeks and purple sweater.

"Yeah," Josh agreed at first, moving to sit down—but then he stopped himself and waved a finger at the girls. "No. Because I sat down the first time and I feel like if I sit down this time, it won't reflect well on me."

"Yeah?" asked rosy cheeks. "How does this reflect on you? If you don't sit down, I will tell every girl on campus that you belong to the bravest girl I have ever met and we will make sure that no one goes out with you the whole time you're here."

"Okay, I'll sit down," Josh finally conceded. "But only because *I* want to."

"Maya, he's seventeen and you're fourteen?" rosy cheeks asked, turning to look into Maya's eyes.

"Yeah." Maya nodded.

"That might seem like a really big age difference now, but here in college, we learn really difficult math," rosy cheeks said with a reassuring smile.

"Yeah, and when you get here, you'll be eighteen and he'll be twenty-one," added purple sweater. "And the good news is that he'll be smarter, because he'll be in college."

"And he just may be smart enough to look at you differently," rosy cheeks concluded.

"Okay!" Josh clapped his hands and rubbed them together. "Thank you, guys, for figuring out my entire life for me—but this has been the worst party of my life." Then he looked kindly at Maya. "C'mon, let's go."

"Oh, you're leaving?" asked rosy cheeks with a knowing grin.

Josh nodded and smiled in spite of himself. "I'm going to walk them home," he confirmed, placing his hand on Maya's back and guiding her and Riley toward the door.

In the hallway, Riley smiled victoriously to herself. But as she walked past the bulletin board, the giant tot burst through a Gamma Gamma Nu poster. "Not so fast, toots!" it called to her.

Spinning around, Riley stared straight into its beady little eyes and insisted, "Don't you start with me! I feel great and there is nothing you can say that will take that away from me!"

"Because you had the best night of your life?" the potato tot jeered.

"Yeah!" Riley nodded.

"And you can't wait to tell your parents?"

"Yeah!"

"If only you hadn't lied to them and snuck out the window," the tot bleated.

"You *know* about that?"

"I know everything. I also know you can't *ever* tell them."

"Oh, yeah." Riley's heart sank as she turned away from the pesky potato and raced to catch up with Maya and Josh.

"Enjoy the rest of your evening!" the tot called after her. "I'll be with you all night."

Riley tried to get away before it could say anything else—but there was no escaping it. The *boom boom* of its awful, menacing little voice continued to echo in her ears, and in her heart, all the way back home. So much for passing the test. So much for *good-bye, conscience—hello, college*. Apparently, she was still the same old Riley after all.

CHAPTER 8

In history class the next morning, Riley was in a state of panic. She hadn't slept the previous night, thanks to the giant potato tot haunting and taunting her. How did Maya do it? How did she do all those things she wasn't supposed to do without ever getting caught, and without giving any of it a second thought?

"This is how you *live*?" Riley finally demanded of her best friend. "You just do bad stuff, and you get away with it?"

"Is something bothering you, darling?" Maya smiled.

As Riley's panic turned to rage, the tot appeared on her left shoulder. "Helloooo!" it bleated.

"Okay, go ahead," Riley fired back at it.

"Your father *trusts* you," the tot cackled, ducking behind Riley's head and popping back up behind her right shoulder. "Your mother *trusts* you." It ducked back down and popped back up on her left. "Your brother *lied* for you," it said, ducking and popping back up again. "Everything bad in the world is your fault."

"*What?*" Riley challenged the annoying tot.

"Never mind, that's for later," the tot replied, quickly disappearing as Mr. Matthews walked into the classroom.

Before he could even make it to his desk, Riley's hand shot up.

"Good morning," said Mr. Matthews.

"What happened to the guy?" Riley blurted out.

"What guy?" Mr. Matthews asked.

"The *Tell-Tale Heart* guy. What happened when his conscience got the better of him?"

But Mr. Matthews didn't get a chance to

respond. Zay beat him to it. "Ohhh, the boom boom guy? Yeah, he went crazy."

"Crazy?" Riley laughed nervously. "What do you mean 'went crazy'?"

"He freaked out from a guilty conscience," Farkle chimed in.

Popping up behind Riley's shoulder, the tot bleated, "Classic."

"How do you get your conscience to stop making you feel guilty?" Riley asked her father.

"Well, the best way is not to do the things you shouldn't do," Mr. Matthews said, leaning against the front of his desk. "But if you do do something wrong—"

"Ha! He said 'doo-doo,'" the tot giggled behind Riley's shoulder.

"—you have to understand that's just your conscience trying to get you to take responsibility for it," Mr. Matthews continued.

"Why?" Riley asked.

"Because when you take responsibility for the things you do, that's when you finally begin to grow," Mr. Matthews revealed, stepping away from his desk.

"So listening to your conscience helps you grow?" Maya asked.

"Yeah." Mr. Matthews smiled down at her. "You might want to try it sometime."

As Maya considered the teacher's words, the giant tot suddenly popped up on her shoulder. "Well, hello, Maya. It's been a long time. . . ."

Maya turned to look at the tot. "What the . . . ?"

As it turned out, Maya had a conscience after all. Now she just needed to figure out what to do with it.

CHAPTER 9

Later that evening, sitting in the bay window of her bedroom with Maya, Riley couldn't take it anymore. She knew what she had to do. But she needed Maya to agree to it first.

"I want to tell my parents what I did," she said.

"Too late," Maya replied.

"I want to tell them how much I'm looking forward to going to college someday," Riley continued.

But Riley's parents had been listening at the door. "Because you loved those college girls you met there?" Mrs. Matthews asked, walking into the room with Mr. Matthews.

"They were so great!" Riley agreed with a faraway look in her eyes. *Wait.* How did her mom know about the college girls? "What?"

"Because one day you hope to be those kinds of girls yourselves?" Mr. Matthews asked.

Riley's apprehension turned to elation when she realized what was going on. "You knew? They knew! Parents know everything!"

"No, someone told us," Mrs. Matthews revealed as Josh walked into the room behind her.

"I just wanted to say good-bye," Josh announced, tossing his duffel bag on the floor. "Very interesting visit."

"Josh." Riley rolled her eyes at her uncle as he sat down between her and Maya. "You told them."

"Told them what, Riley?" Josh looked at her sideways. "That nothing happened? Why would I tell them nothing happened if nothing happened? Why would I tell them that, huh?"

"It's okay, Josh." Mr. Matthews smiled. "Maya told us."

"What?" Riley turned to look at her best friend.

"Maya told us everything," Mrs. Matthews confirmed.

"Why?" Riley couldn't believe it was true.

"I wouldn't rat you out, Riley," Josh interjected, turning to smile at Mr. Matthews. "Sorry, Cory. Guess I'm still your little brother, huh?"

Mr. Matthews shook his head sympathetically. "No, Josh. I mean, you were so looking forward to making new friends at that party, but you left just to make sure Riley and Maya got home safely. You're not so little anymore, Josh. I guess I have to stop looking at you that way."

"Thanks." Josh beamed with pride. "That means a lot to me."

Riley was floored—and confused. "Maya. Why did you tell them?"

"It's a choice I made for myself," Maya confessed softly. "I thought it was the grown-up thing to do."

Josh looked at her in awe. "It was. You're not so little anymore, Maya. I guess I have to stop looking at you that way."

"Thanks." Maya smiled coyly. "That means a lot to me."

"Riley," Mrs. Matthews said, turning to look at her daughter, "are you ever going to pull something like this again?"

"No," Riley insisted. "Even though it may have been a great night, it isn't worth how terrible I feel for not telling you."

Just then, the tot reappeared on Riley's shoulder. "Thanks," it bleated. "That means a lot to me."

A little while later, after Josh had departed, Riley was still talking through the previous night's adventures with Maya and her family.

"Riley, we're happy that you liked your college experience—" Mrs. Matthews began.

"And we're sad to have to give you a grounding experience," Mr. Matthews continued, holding up a pair of fingers. "Two weeks."

"It should be three," taunted the potato tot,

Hey, Maya here! Riley's uncle Josh, aka "Uncle Boing," is gonna go to college in New York City!

You love him. —Riley

Guess who tried to play it cool and failed? Hint: She's short and blonde, and her name rhymes with "Hiya!"

At least my name doesn't rhyme with "Smiley"!

Maya was
determined to
go to Josh's
college party.

And Riley was
determined to
keep me out of
trouble.

Zay knew all about that creepy
Tell-Tale Heart book.   BOOM, BOOM!

We left fake Riley in my bed so that my parents wouldn't know I was gone. I'M a genius.

My guilty ~~tot~~ conscience made me want to confess. . . .

Cute or creepy? You decide.

And then this happened.
We TOT-ally knew you had a conscience, Maya!

Farkle and Maya were trying to make me and Lucas uncomfortable by talking about kissing . . . and it worked.

Baaahaahaaa!

Look at Riley, all embarrassed. Stop it.

This is an exact reenactment of the kiss between Riley and Lucas. Stop it!

Here's where our friends forced us into dating.
It's true.

And the award for Most Awkward
Couple goes to . . .
Srsly.

I guess you could say it was a day of awkward couples.

In my defense, I was blinded by the bling.

Topanga convinced them to break up.

It was more like conscious uncoupling.

which had set up shop on the table next to the window seat.

"Deal," Riley said to her parents, ignoring the annoying nugget.

"It should be three!" the tot repeated.

"Get a life!" Riley snapped at the tot. Just then, her little brother walked into the room in his green striped jammies.

"Good night," Auggie said sweetly. "I brushed my teeth."

"You did not," replied the tot.

Auggie shot a confused look at the end table. "What the . . . ?"

"Auggie," Mrs. Matthews said, picking up her son and setting him on the window seat cushions between her and Riley. "You are grounded for one week for not telling us your sister snuck out of the house."

"How is that a bad thing?" Auggie protested. "I was protecting her."

Satisfied that its work there was done—for the

moment, anyway—the tot turned to look at Maya. "Let's go, blondie. You and I are gonna do a little growin' up together."

Maya frowned. "We're gonna tell my mother, aren't we?"

"We're gonna tell her about a *lot* of stuff," the tot replied.

"Yeah, okay, let's go," Maya agreed with a sigh, picking up the tot and setting it on her shoulder before turning to wave good-bye to the Matthewses. "See you guys in a year!"

As Riley waved to her best friend—and the potato tot—a sense of victory washed over her again. But it felt different this time. She hadn't won because she'd gotten away with something. She'd won because she was taking responsibility for it. She'd listened to her conscience and grown. But even better than that? Her best friend had done the same thing. They were going to be so ready for college when the time finally came!

CHAPTER 1

As they sat in the bay window of her room before school, Riley could tell that Maya was in a bit of a mood—and Riley was pretty sure she knew why. Ever since Riley's first official date with Lucas, Maya had been trying to get Riley to talk about what had happened—but Riley didn't want to talk about it. Well, it wasn't that she didn't *want* to talk about it. It was more like she didn't know *how* to talk about it.

"How long are we avoiding this?" Maya demanded.

"Not avoiding nothin'," Riley insisted. "Just

life moving on beyond that thing that happened between me and Lucas."

Maya pursed her full lips and teased Riley with a kissy face and smooching sound.

"I know what it was, you do not have to fish-face at me!" Riley sighed.

But Maya wouldn't give it up. She brought her hands up to her cheeks and squashed them to make an even more exaggerated kissy face with even louder smooching noises.

Riley rolled her eyes and shook her head. "Maya, other things are happening. Life got over it. Why can't you?"

"Life isn't over it," Maya lamented. "Haven't you noticed everything has stopped? Nothing's happening."

"Everything's happening!" Riley flung out her arms, making a grand gesture toward her room, her face lighting up enthusiastically. Alas . . . *crickets*. So she and Maya sat there and stared at the ground for what felt like hours, until the silence was broken with more of Maya's pestering.

"Riley, until we talk about"—again with the kissy face and smooching noises—"nothing's ever happening again."

Riley shook her head. "Ohhh, that's the talk of a *kook*!"

Honestly. It wasn't like there weren't other important things to talk about. Every day was practically bursting at the seams with places to go, people to see, things to do. Riley leaned forward, anticipating a moment of extreme excitement to hit them any . . . minute . . . now!

More crickets.

Maya sighed loudly as they both sat there, glancing around the room, hands crossed in their laps. Finally, a face appeared in the open window.

"Ladies!" Farkle crooned.

"Yay!" Riley bounced up and down and wrapped her arms around her friend, squeezing him tight.

"Well, *that's* settled, then," Farkle gasped in amazement and delight, savoring every moment of Riley's embrace.

But Maya wasn't happy about the interruption.

"Are you here for a reason, Farkle?" she asked impatiently.

"I've got two tickets to a concert, but there's three of us," he whined. "So who do I take?"

"You see?" Riley turned to look at Maya. "That right there is a very original situation. There will be many twists and turns that no one will see coming!"

"I liked the way you hugged me, Riley. I'm taking you," Farkle quickly concluded, ducking away from the window and disappearing.

Riley dropped her jaw in exaggerated surprise. "I did not see that coming," she swore, shaking her head at Maya.

"So we're back!" Maya declared, eagerly smacking her hands together. She recounted the scene: "Subway car. You lock eyes. You fall into his lap. You grab Lucas by the face. You start moving toward him and—"

"Riley!" Mr. Matthews burst through the door with Riley's mom beside him. He didn't always have the best timing, but at that moment, it was pretty darn impeccable.

"Yay! Did I do something? Am I grounded? Does she have to leave?" Riley's words tumbled out of her mouth in an enthusiastic torrent as she turned to look at Maya and frowned apologetically. "You have to leave."

"No, we're glad you're both here," Mrs. Matthews said. "We need you to babysit Auggie."

"They need us to babysit Auggie!" Riley raved, certain this was precisely what was needed to steer Maya's focus in a new—and much better—direction.

But instead, Maya practically yawned in Riley's face. "Been there, done that."

"*Things could happen twice!*" Riley insisted.

Mrs. Matthews didn't like the sound of that. "Unless it's an emergency, we don't want to hear from you," she warned them.

"What could happen?" Riley wondered, her voice dropping dramatically as she searched her mind for some solid possibilities. "I'll tell you!

We'll put too much soap in the washing machine and then we'll find a puppy and say, 'Can we keep him?' and then his owner will show up. It'll be this hot guy that Maya will totally like—"

"Yayyy!" At long last, Maya hopped on Riley's imaginary wild ride.

"But he'll move away because Maya can never be happy—" Riley continued.

"Booo!" Maya frowned.

"You see?" Riley shot a sly grin at her best friend. "We got a lot going on today!"

"Tomorrow," Mr. Matthews said, correcting her.

"Huh?" Riley wrinkled up her nose.

"Yeah, we need you to babysit tomorrow," Mrs. Matthews told her.

"Today we got nothin'," Mr. Matthews added with a lame shrug as he and Riley's mom spun around and left the room.

"So!" Maya growled eagerly without skipping a beat. "You got Lucas by the face and—"

"Help me!" Auggie begged, marching through the doorway.

"Yay! Auggie!" Riley leapt up and raced over to pick up her perfect, cherubic little brother, then carried him back to the window seat and plunked him down between her and Maya. "Do you have any problems that I can help you with?"

"Well, I made a new friend at school," Auggie began, his voice full of worry as he turned from Riley to Maya and back to Riley. "What if Mom doesn't like him? What if she picks him up and puts him in the hallway like Ava? What if no one is ever good enough for Mommy's little boy?"

Riley wrapped an arm around Auggie and ruffled his thick dark curls. "This is a thing!" She tossed a triumphant smile at Maya.

"Ehh. Not a *whole* thing." Maya crossed her legs and shook her long blond hair indifferently. "We check back on this twice, tops."

"I would be involved in it!" Riley insisted.

But Maya shook her head and stared at the ceiling. "Completely your mother's thing."

Riley considered that for a moment. Maya had a point. Why did she have to be right about this?

"Yeah." She frowned at her little brother. "Scram."

Auggie slowly got up from the window seat and marched out of the room, shouting, "Moooommmmm!" as he made his way down the hall.

Then it was just Maya and Riley. Riley and Maya. Sitting there on the old, familiar window seat. Nothing to say. Nothing to see. Nothing to do. "So . . . that's everybody we know, huh?" Riley forced a tight smile.

"Not quite," Maya replied. "You've got one more friend who has a problem you can get involved in."

"I do? Who?" Riley would take anyone at that point.

Maya smiled and raised her hand.

"Oh, yeah!" Riley grinned, sliding a little closer and linking arms with Maya as she practically cheered, "My troubled, misunderstood friend. People *love* your problems! You're a *mess*!"

"Thanks," Maya grumbled. "My problem is that I have a best friend who doesn't want to talk about the most important thing going on in her life and I don't know what to do. Can you help me, please?"

Ugh. There it was. No more tiptoeing around the subject. Maya had whacked her right over the head with it. *Fine*. "I kissed Lucas," Riley finally said, swallowing the lump in her throat. Saying the words out loud was enough to fill her entire belly with butterflies.

"You don't say!" Maya sounded so giddy, so relieved.

If only Riley could feel the same sense of calm. "What happens now?" she asked softly, searching her best friend's eyes for some sort of reassurance.

It was the question she'd avoided asking herself, not to mention Lucas, ever since that night on the subway. But she knew she was going to have to figure it out eventually. Even if she wasn't quite ready for the answer, apparently Maya couldn't wait.

CHAPTER 2

Later that day, at school, Riley wasn't any closer to knowing what was going to happen between her and Lucas. All she knew was that things had changed. They were in uncharted territory, and at some point they were going to have to learn how to interact with each other in a whole new way. Fortunately, they were also going to have to learn what her dad was about to start teaching the class— meaning Riley could push her uncertain future with Lucas to the back of her mind again. For now.

"The New World," said Mr. Matthews, standing in front of the chalkboard, where he'd written *ELLIS ISLAND: IMMIGRATION*. "People who lived their whole lives in a certain place traveled to a new land of new feelings and new opportunities, having no idea how to behave in this brand-new society."

What the . . . ? Yet again, Riley's dad seemed to have been eavesdropping on her thoughts—and this didn't sound like a history lesson so much as a play-by-play of everything that was happening between her and Lucas! With heat quickly rising to her cheeks, Riley spun around to look at Lucas, who was already shooting an equally confused and concerned look back at her.

"Lucas, what did you tell him?" Riley loud-whispered after turning back around in her seat, avoiding his stare.

"Nothing. I. Am. Also. Uncomfortable." Lucas spoke like an awkward robot version of himself.

Ever the astute observer, Farkle looked at Maya and whispered, "Wait, Mr. Matthews doesn't know Riley kissed Lucas?"

"Nope," Maya replied with eager delight.

"So everything he says is making them uncomfortable?"

"Uh-huh." Maya was grinning from ear to ear.

"Shall we take advantage of this?" Farkle wondered aloud.

"How could we not?" Maya agreed.

"I will begin!" Farkle jumped up from his chair and addressed the teacher. "So, Mr. Matthews. Tell me. After you've had the courage to close your eyes and take the face of the New World in your trembling hands . . ." He raised his hands, closed his eyes tight, and puckered up.

Oh, dear. Oh, my. What is Farkle doing? Riley wondered as she let out a pained little "yeep."

Apparently, Mr. Matthews was wondering the same thing. "What are you trying to say, Farkle?" he asked, squinting at the auburn-haired brainiac.

"Are you supposed to be a couple next or what?" Farkle blurted out.

"Huh?" Mr. Matthews scrunched up his face, completely lost.

"What?" Riley gasped, nowhere near as lost as she wanted to be.

"Huh?" Lucas glared at Farkle.

"Oh, you don't understand my question?" Farkle looked from Lucas to Maya and extended his arms toward her. "Perhaps my dear friend Ms. Maya Penelope Hart could help me out. . . ."

The moment Maya's middle name shot out of Farkle's mouth, a combination of fear and anger flashed across her face.

"Penelope!" taunted their classmate Sarah, her eyes dancing with amusement behind thick-framed glasses as she grinned at Maya.

"Farkle!" Maya scowled.

"It came out! It just came out! It came out! It just came out!" Farkle stammered apologetically, collapsing back into his chair.

"Penelope?" Lucas smirked at his desk behind Maya's, clearly thrilled that he finally had something he could tease her about.

Maya spun around in her chair and stared him down. "Really, Huckleberry, you wanna play with me right now?"

"No." Lucas instantly backed off.

"'Cause you've done *quite* enough, haven't you?"

Maya continued, leaning over Lucas's desk and puckering up her lips at him.

"Maya." Lucas glared at her.

"Maya," Riley added firmly.

"Mr. Matthews." Maya spun back around, her lips curled in an eager grin. "I think what Farkle is trying to say is, once you've kissed—"

"Yeep," Riley squeaked.

"—the shores of this new world, I bet your friends from the Old World would want to hear about how the New World is, and if you don't tell them, well, that's just selfish!"

Luckily for Riley, Mr. Matthews was still lost. "What are you trying to say, Penelope?"

"Are you supposed to be a couple or what?" Maya demanded.

"All right," Mr. Matthews said, exasperated, "what's going on here, guys?"

"Nothing!" Riley insisted, fumbling around on her desk. "Could we just for once read from the book?" She opened to a chapter in the middle and quickly began reading. "'The boy and girl had no idea of the changes they would soon be facing. Everything around them was different, including their own bodies.'" Riley stopped abruptly when the words registered in her brain. "What the . . . ?"

Maya stifled a laugh. "You're reading your health book."

Farkle held up a finger and shot a terrified look at Riley. "Word of warning—page seventy-three. I don't understand it! It makes no sense! It looks impossible!"

Mr. Matthews had had enough. "Riley! What is going on here?" he asked again.

"Farkle kissed my hand!" Maya volunteered in a noble effort to cover for her best friend.

"You did?" Mr. Matthews looked impressed as he glanced at Farkle.

"It was glorious." Farkle sighed.

"It was," Maya agreed, keeping up the charade. "I went home and questioned everything."

"Okay." Mr. Matthews nodded and took a few steps toward Riley's desk. "And where were you when all of this hand kissing was going on?"

"Nowhere with no one doing nothing with nobody!" Riley said forcefully, staring straight ahead and avoiding her father's eyes.

Mr. Matthews tilted his head, examining his daughter as if she was a science experiment. Then he slowly and deliberately walked to Lucas and examined him. Lucas looked back at Mr. Matthews as innocently as possible but then jumped straight out of his chair and raced from the classroom, climbing over students and desks as he made his escape. Mr. Matthews walked back to Riley and continued to examine her from every possible angle.

Unable to take another uncomfortable moment, Riley turned to Maya, desperate to make her own escape. "Auggie now."

Shrugging, Maya finally relented. "I don't see where else we can go."

If only focusing on her little brother's problems could make Riley's disappear. But somehow she knew it wouldn't be quite that easy.

CHAPTER 3

Back at the Matthews apartment, Auggie was excited to have his new friend over to play. He silently hoped that his mom would stay at the kitchen table doing her lawyer work while he did his own work making sure they had fun.

"I'm sorry I didn't have time to buy you something before you came over," Auggie said as they sat on the couch in the living room.

"You don't have to buy me something," his friend replied.

Auggie was so used to his kinda-sorta girlfriend,

Ava, from down the hall, demanding gifts that he was a bit confused by this. "Why else would you come over?"

"I came to play with you."

Mrs. Matthews had been so busy working she'd hardly noticed that Mr. Matthews had brought Auggie and his friend home. But when she caught the tail end of their conversation, she rushed to the couch and plopped herself down between the boys. "Auggie! Who's your nice normal friend who isn't Ava and doesn't need gifts to come over and play with you?"

"Doy!" Auggie's friend replied, looking up at Mrs. Matthews with his sweet brown puppy-dog eyes.

"Excuse me?" Mrs. Matthews stared at the boy like he'd just sprouted a second head.

Auggie immediately grabbed his mother by the shoulder. "Leave it alone, Mom," he begged.

But Mrs. Matthews wasn't known for leaving things alone. "Okay, wait a minute, though. Your name, again? Will you just spell that for me?"

"D-e-w-e-y," the boy replied, then crossed his little arms before boldly concluding, "Doy."

"Wait a minute." Mrs. Matthews stared harder at Auggie's friend, as if yet another head had sprouted.

"The 'w' is silent," Dewey explained, batting his lashes.

"Let it be silent," Auggie implored his mom. "He's my first bro."

Mrs. Matthews plastered on her sweetest smile as she looked from Auggie to Dewey. "Okay, but see, honey, the 'w' is actually . . . not . . . silent."

"No!" Dewey shrieked.

"Yes," Mrs. Matthews insisted.

"*Doyyy!*" the little boy screamed, flinging out his arms defiantly.

"Let him be right, Mom," Auggie commanded.

"Except he's *not* right." Mrs. Matthews, still smiling sweetly, looked from Auggie to Dewey.

"No, see, his name is not Doyyy. It's *Dewey*! With a 'w'... that you *say*."

That was absolutely not what Dewey wanted to hear. Staring into Mrs. Matthews's face, he looked like he'd just been punched in the gut and began to hyperventilate. *"Hihh—hiih—"*

"Wh-wha-what is that?" Mrs. Matthews began to panic a bit herself. "What are you doing?"

Dewey's wheezing suddenly erupted into an explosive, uncontrollable scream so loud that his entire face turned as red as the stripes on his hooded sweatshirt, causing Mrs. Matthews and Auggie to lean back in shock.

"You ruined my playdate!" Auggie yelled at his mom, throwing his hands up in frustration.

"I'm sorry!" Mrs. Matthews looked at her poor little boy and then stared into the teary eyes of his friend. "I'm so sorry, Dewey."

"DOYYYYYY!" he screamed so loudly that Mrs. Matthews and Auggie nearly fell off the couch.

Hearing the screams, Mr. Matthews raced into

the living room to see what was wrong. "What the . . . ?" He turned to look at Mrs. Matthews. "What'd you do to Doy?"

Mrs. Matthews did a double take. Had her husband just said what she thought he'd said? "Are you kidding me, Cory?"

But Mr. Matthews had already gotten to know Auggie's new friend quite well. "It's Coy," he told his wife firmly. "Around him, it's Coy." Then, turning to Dewey and kneeling down, he threw his arms open wide and added, "Come to Coy, Doy."

Dewey raced to the safe haven of Mr. Matthews's arms. "Can we go to Auggie's room?" the little boy sobbed.

"Yes!" Mr. Matthews agreed, on the verge of tears himself as he grabbed the little boy's hand. "I'll go and read you a stoy."

With that, Mr. Matthews led Auggie and his friend out of the room, leaving Mrs. Matthews all alone. She shook her head and crossed her arms, marveling at the scene she'd just witnessed. What had happened to her husband? What had happened to her son? How could they possibly go along with Dewey on this? She was not going to let it go that easily. She needed some answers.

CHAPTER 4

After school, Riley grabbed her books from her locker, desperate to make her escape with Maya and get home to Auggie and his problems. But when she spun around to leave, she discovered a huge crowd of girls staring at her like wild animals stalking their prey.

"Everybody stop looking at me!" Riley scowled.

"Tell us." Sarah leaned in eagerly.

"I don't kiss and tell," Riley replied.

"Didja kiss?" Darby widened her blue eyes, ready for all the details.

"Yes," Riley admitted before realizing what she was saying.

"Tell!" Darby insisted.

"And take your time," Sarah added with a mischievous grin.

Riley leaned back against her locker and frowned. It was none of their business. "Nothing happened," she told them, extending an arm to tap her best friend on the shoulder. "Back me up, Maya."

But instead of complying, Maya turned to face the lockers, her back to the crowd of girls as she wrapped her arms around herself and launched into a fake making-out act, prompting all the girls to giggle.

"That's inaccurate," Riley said, pointing at Maya.

So Maya spun around, pushed her palms to her cheeks, and did the whole kissy-face, smooching-noises thing.

Okay, fine. Riley couldn't resist a smile as she motioned to Maya and said, "Yeah, that's pretty good."

Meanwhile, on the opposite side of the indoor quad, Lucas sat next to Farkle and attempted to fight off his own swarm of wild animal stalkers.

"So, what's the next thing you guys are supposed to do?" Farkle asked. The crowd of guys behind them leaned in a little closer.

"Supposed to do?" Lucas shook his head. "What are there, rules?"

"I don't know, but I don't see how you can just kiss someone and not be with them after. I only kissed Maya's hand," Farkle noted, pulling out a small velvet box, "and then I got her this engagement ring right after we got off the subway."

The enormous rock Farkle had produced immediately made every single guy's jaw drop. Lucas took the box and stared at the ring, mesmerized.

"Ohmygosh, Farkle," he gasped. "How much was that?"

"Seventy-eight thousand dollars. But I got it for free."

"How?" Lucas demanded.

"Because that's the ring my mom keeps throwing

at my father!" Farkle smiled and took the box from Lucas. "She usually wants it back by Thursday, so I gotta work fast."

At the lockers, Riley continued to field questions from the girls. It was like she was holding a press conference or something.

"So, are you guys boyfriend and girlfriend now, or what are you?" Sarah's eyes lit up behind her glasses.

"What are you?" Darby chimed in, shaking her long platinum-blond hair.

Riley felt a bit queasy at the thought of being boyfriend and girlfriend. These were the exact questions she'd been trying to avoid! "I don't know, do we have to be something?"

"Well, you did kiss him," Sarah pointed out.

"What are you?" Darby asked again.

"Look"—Maya walked over to the crowd of girls to set them straight—"it just happened. She's not really sure what it all means yet."

But apparently, Darby had her own romantic plans for Riley and Lucas. "You guys are meant to be together. Like me and Yogi!" Spying her tiny dark-haired boyfriend walking past the bank of lockers, the tall blonde squealed, "Yogles!" He rushed over and leapt into her arms, and she raced off with him.

Riley stared after the odd couple. "Will Lucas and I ever have what they have?" she wondered.

"Boy, I hope not." Maya grimaced as she turned to look at her best friend. "You know, Riles, they do have a point. I mean, you like him, he likes you, there was a kiss. . . ."

"I will not act under peer pressure," Riley insisted. But then, thinking a bit more about it, she added, "Unless you think I should."

When she said that, the girls all rushed over, intent on making sure that Riley and Lucas became a couple. They all seemed to have so much invested in the situation—and suddenly, Riley felt like she couldn't possibly let them down.

On the other side of the quad, the boys were pushing Lucas to make things official with Riley, too—but he was resisting just as much.

"I will not give in to peer pressure!" Lucas told them.

"What if we carry you?" Farkle asked.

"I'd like to see you try."

"Darby!" Farkle called out, causing their surprisingly strong classmate to turn away from her conversation with Yogi. She raced over to help Farkle pick up Lucas, and they carried him to where Riley was standing.

"What are you?" Darby asked again as she set Lucas down.

"What are we?" Riley said softly, turning to look at Lucas.

"Are we boyfriend and girlfriend?" Lucas didn't sound very sure.

"Are we?" Riley felt even less sure than she sounded.

Lucas blinked a few times. "I dunno, you wanna?"

"I don't know. You think, maybe?" Riley blinked back.

Lucas swallowed a big lump in his throat and finally said again, "Wanna?"

"Are they weird or adorable?" Sarah wondered out loud.

"No," Darby replied, throwing an arm around her little boyfriend and smiling blissfully. "Me and Yogi are weird. They're adorable."

Riley's vision became a bit blurry as she looked at Lucas. "What just happened?" she asked, turning to look at Maya and Farkle, who were standing between her and Lucas. "Do I have my first boyfriend?"

"I don't know," Farkle replied with a satisfied, eager smile. "What just happened?"

"I don't know." Maya's smile was even bigger than Farkle's. "Can't wait to see what happens next."

But before Riley even had a chance to think about where to go from there, Farkle dropped down on one knee and presented Maya with a giant sparkling engagement ring. Everyone in the quad stared at the diamond, but nobody was more mesmerized by it than Maya, who swayed back and forth as Farkle waved it up at her.

Wait a minute! Just as Riley was finally preparing for this strange new journey with Lucas—finally ready to get answers to all the questions that had come up since that night on the subway—Farkle was popping a humongous question of his own?

But once the initial shock of Farkle's proposal wore off, the focus was back on Riley and Lucas. There they sat, still surrounded by their classmates, heads spinning with way more questions than answers.

"Okay, here we are," Riley said, trying to talk her way through nervous energy. "What do we do now?"

"You go on a date after school," Sarah replied as if it was the most obvious thing in the world.

"You sit there and look at each other all stupid— like this," Darby added, turning to gaze into Yogi's eyes as they exchanged the goofiest grins ever.

"Stop," Lucas said as much to Darby as to the

rest of their classmates. "Nobody's telling us what to do. We're not *you*. *You're* you. We're *us*. *We* do what *we* do."

"Yeah! We do what *we* do!" Riley was relieved that Lucas had it all figured out. Now she just needed him to help *her* figure it out. She leaned into him and whispered, "What do we do?"

But Lucas stared blankly at Riley, and she stared blankly back at him. Eventually, they decided that maybe following Sarah's and Darby's advice wasn't such a bad thing. So, fine. They would go on a date after school. They would sit there and stare at each other all stupid—at least, until they came up with some better answers of their own. It had to happen eventually. Riley was *almost* sure of it.

CHAPTER 5

Sitting at the kitchen table with her husband and Auggie, Mrs. Matthews was trying hard to get some answers to her questions about why they were so quick to accept Dewey as Doy. But Mr. Matthews had some questions of his own.

"What is it in you that makes you do this?" he demanded of his wife.

"His name is Dewey!" Mrs. Matthews fired back.

"What's the difference what his name is?" Mr. Matthews fumed, shaking his hands in frustration. "He says his name is Doy and he wants to be called Doy. So we call him Doy, because he says his name is Doy. And Doy is a guest in our house. So will you please let go of your need to be right all the time, and we just call the kid Doy?"

As Mrs. Matthews turned away from her husband, unable to let it go, a tiny voice at the kitchen doorway asked meekly, "Doy?"

They all turned around to look at little Dewey, whose face was still stained with tears, lips still trembling.

Pasting her sweet Mommy smile back on, Mrs. Matthews asked the little boy, "Can I please talk to you for a minute?"

But he stayed right where he was, eyes wide with terror, and looked at Mr. Matthews and Auggie for guidance.

"I wouldn't," Auggie warned his friend.

"I wouldn't, either," Mr. Matthews muttered, staring down at the table.

But Mrs. Matthews could be pretty convincing. "Come here," she coaxed him, holding out her arms.

Dewey took a few tentative steps toward her. Then a few more. He still looked terrified, but at long last he got close enough that Mrs. Matthews was able to pick him up and set him on her lap.

"Okay," she told him, "here's what's going to happen next."

She wasn't ready to give up completely, but Mrs. Matthews realized that a softer approach would probably be more effective. If there was one thing she'd learned in all her years of being a lawyer, it was that to get the answers you wanted, you had to ask the right questions—in the right way.

CHAPTER 6

Riley's heart was pounding and her palms were sweating as she and Lucas sat in two matching orange chairs at Topanga's, the café her mom had inherited from Mrs. Svorski. Finally, breaking the awkward silence, the waitress brought over the smoothie Lucas had ordered for them.

"One smoothie, two straws," she announced, setting the drink down on a gold napkin on the coffee table in front of them.

Lucas looked up at the server with a blank, quiet stare.

"You two new at this?" she asked, and he nodded dizzily up at her. "Don't worry. It gets harder."

As the waitress walked away, Riley couldn't imagine *anything* being harder. Lucas was sitting mere inches away from her, but it felt like he was on another planet. Not only did he seem like a stranger; he seemed like a complete *alien.*

"We're just sitting here," she finally said out loud.

"Yeah." Lucas sighed. "We haven't talked to each other much at all."

Riley stole a quick sideways glance. "It's too bad, because you're one of my favorite people to talk to."

But Lucas wouldn't even look at her. Instead, his eyes darted to the old bookcases, to the college kids drinking coffee and eating muffins at the counter. "I think your mom did a really good job on this place."

"Yeah." Riley smiled as she noticed all the couples sitting at tables, engrossed in conversation. "Gonna be a great hangout, isn't it?"

"Yeah." Lucas nodded and finally peeked at Riley for a moment before turning away again. "Look at all these NYU students. Smiling . . ."

"Talking," Riley added.

"Looking real . . ." Lucas paused.

"Comfortable with each other. Yeah," Riley concluded, chewing on her lower lip.

"Yeah." Finally, Lucas turned and looked directly at Riley. "I don't know why it's so hard for us to talk all of a sudden. It's not like we've changed."

"We're boyfriend and girlfriend now," Riley pointed out.

"Yeah, but those are just words, Riley. Words don't change people."

Hmmm. Riley had to think about that one. But before she had a chance to let it sink in, Maya and Farkle arrived.

"Mrs. Farkle Minkus," Maya announced, extending her arm toward Riley so she could observe the blinding rock on Maya's finger.

"You said *yes*?" Riley couldn't hide her shock.

Maya practically danced over to where Farkle was sitting, never taking her gaze away from the ring as she fell onto the antique chaise next to him and declared, "Good-bye, Maya Penelope Hart—hello, Mrs. Farkle Minkus."

Farkle gazed lovingly at his "fiancée." "All this time I've been trying to love and appreciate her and all it took was this big honkin' rock."

Riley and Lucas exchanged confused glances. There was no way this was really happening.

"Make a note, Riley," Maya instructed, still 100 percent focused on the ring. "They put one of these in front of our face and we get hypnotized by the sparkles."

"Wait." Farkle tried to get Maya's attention. "You only said yes because of the ring? It had nothing to do with me?"

Finally, Maya tore her gaze away from the ring to look at Farkle. "That would be pretty shallow of me, wouldn't it?"

"I don't care." Farkle grinned.

But Maya found that troubling. "All right, Farkle, you're a scientist. Let's do an experiment." She removed the ring from her finger and handed it back to him. "Ask me without the ring."

"Would you marry me?" Farkle quickly asked her.

"Die," came Maya's immediate response. "Now ask me with the ring."

Farkle held out the ring to Maya and asked again, "Would you marry me?"

"I love you so much!" Maya practically sobbed—to the ring.

"I believe you!" Farkle beamed.

Maya put the ring back on her finger, unable to stop staring at it. "Hypnotized, Riley. You need to protect me."

"Protect you from what, Maya?" Riley was a bit worried about her friend. "Relationships are supposed to be about two people who make the choice to come together by themselves."

"Of their own free will," Lucas added. "At the right point in time."

"It has nothing to do with—" Before Riley could finish her thought, Maya was waving her hand so Riley could get a good, long look at the ring. *Wow.* It really was kind of hypnotic. "How do they get these things so sparkly, Farkly?" Riley murmured.

"Pressure," Farkle replied. "This diamond used to just be a piece of coal that was put under a lot of pressure."

"Yeah." Maya nodded and gazed lovingly down at the ring again. "I'm keeping it."

"Good. I come with it," Farkle informed her.

"Huh." Maya scrunched up her face, still gazing down at the ring. "Well, I really love you and everything."

"Why, thank you!" Farkle smiled.

"I was talking to the ring," Maya said.

"Oh."

"The way I see it, the only way we could be happy is if I sell you, get a nice house where the two of us would just be happy with each other." Maya ticked off each point in logical order.

"Just me and you?" Farkle nodded eagerly.

"Just me and the ring," Maya said, correcting him.

"Wait. You're selling *me*?"

"I thought that was clear."

"Fine." Farkle shook his head. "Come on, Lucas, let's get outta here."

"Oh." Lucas looked at Riley. "Well, I was gonna walk Riley home."

"You don't have to," Riley told him.

"No, I think I should," he insisted.

Riley forced a smile. She didn't want him to walk her home out of some sense of duty. "Try again."

"I want to very much." That sounded a little more convincing.

"Wait," Maya interjected. "That means I'm walking home with Farkle?"

"You're wearing my ring!" Farkle reminded her.

"Boy, the stuff you gotta do," Maya muttered, shaking her head as she and Farkle made their way out the door.

Riley couldn't help laughing. "I'm not sure it's going to work out with them."

"You think?" Lucas laughed, too.

"So, you're walking me home?" Riley asked, glancing at the door as a college couple entered, holding hands.

"Yeah," Lucas said, also noticing the couple. "Hold hands?"

Yikes. That sounded so serious! "I guess we should," Riley finally said with a gulp.

"Try again." Lucas smirked.

Okay. She could do this. "I want to very much."

Lucas smiled and held out his hand. Riley took a deep breath and grabbed hold of it. They stood up and made their way outside—and were met with a chorus of *oooooohhhhh*s, because as it turned out, all their classmates had followed them.

"Yeah, this isn't going to be weird at all," Riley noted, glancing at Lucas.

Even though he gave her a reassuring smile and guided her up the steps, Riley couldn't shake the feeling that they were heading in the wrong direction. This uncharted territory was even more confusing than she had anticipated, and she still had many unanswered questions. More than ever before.

CHAPTER 7

With Dewey sitting on her lap, Mrs. Matthews looked into his scared brown eyes and began her line of kinder, gentler questioning.

"Do you know what my name is?" she asked.

"Auggie's mommy," Dewey replied carefully.

"Topanga!" Mrs. Matthews told him, widening her eyes dramatically.

But Dewey wasn't going to be swayed that easily. "You're just trying to make me feel better."

"You think *you* have a funny name?" Mrs. Matthews tried again. "I have a funny name, too. When I was a little girl, I could never understand why my parents would do that to me."

Finally, Dewey smiled at her for the first time all afternoon. "I know, right?" he said, and Mr. Matthews and Auggie both began to relax a bit, too.

"But then I found out that they loved me very much," Mrs. Matthews continued. "And they gave me a name that was important to them. Do you know what your name means?"

Dewey shook his head and looked up expectantly, ready for the story.

"Every morning, before the sun comes up, the ground is wet," Mrs. Matthews told him. "And that water is a gift for the flowers and the grass so that they can grow and make the world more beautiful. You were given your name because you make your parents' world more beautiful. Do you understand me?"

Dewey nodded, captivated. At long last, it was time for Mrs. Matthews to go in for the big win— and to finally rest her case.

"And do you know what that water is called that's there for the grass every morning before you wake up?" she asked the little boy.

"Yes." He nodded, the whole thing finally making sense.

"What is it?" Mrs. Matthews couldn't wait for his answer.

"Morning doy."

Auggie and Mr. Matthews cringed, and Mrs. Matthews sighed. So there it was. All those questions, all that effort—for nothing.

"Okay, get outta here, Doy." Mrs. Matthews finally relented and gave the boy a gentle pat.

"Yayyy!" Dewey and Auggie squealed, leaping up from the table and racing to Auggie's room to play.

Mr. Matthews looked at his wife sympathetically. "He broke you."

"Yeah, he did." Mrs. Matthews frowned, defeated, elbows on the table and fingers drumming her cheek.

"You know, Topanga," Mr. Matthews said, puffing out his chest, "one of the things that I've learned from being a teacher is that sometimes you just have to let kids live."

As they both sat and reflected on that for a moment, the front door opened and Riley and Lucas walked into the apartment.

"Thank you very much, Lucas," Riley said in a strained voice. "I had a wonderful time."

Mr. and Mrs. Matthews looked at the pair. Although Riley and Lucas were holding hands, their arms were completely stretched out, as if they couldn't stand to get too close to each other.

"You're welcome, Riley," Lucas replied, struggling with each word. "I also had a wonderful time, as well."

"Uhhh, what are you kids doing?" Mrs. Matthews asked. "You guys look really awkward and stiff. Is this about that kiss I heard about?"

"What?" Mr. Matthews shouted, stunned, as Mrs. Matthews got up and walked across the living room.

"Is everybody pressuring you to be something you're not ready for?" Mrs. Matthews continued.

"Not ready!" Mr. Matthews yelled.

"Please," Mrs. Matthews begged when she

arrived at the door, where Riley and Lucas were standing. "Stop holding hands. You look crazy."

Riley and Lucas couldn't let go quickly enough.

"You two are a part of the best group of friends I have ever seen," Mrs. Matthews told them, crossing her arms. "And if you're going to let some stupid outside pressure hurt that, then you're not anywhere near as smart as I thought you were."

Riley stared into her mother's eyes, eager for more answers. "But sometimes the right pressure can turn you into a diamond," she said tentatively.

"Yeah," Mrs. Matthews agreed. "And the wrong pressure turns you into dust. Do you want to be dust?"

Riley glanced at Lucas and then back at her mother. She shook her head. "I don't want to be dust." She turned to look at Lucas again. "Lucas?"

"I really like you, Riley," he told her.

Riley liked hearing him say that. "We always have such a great time together," she added.

After a long pause, Lucas concluded, "We should break up."

Most girls might have been crushed by that, but it was the first thing that had made sense to Riley all day. "We should break up right now!" she agreed, her heart about to burst with excitement. "This has been my longest relationship."

Lucas grinned. "Hey, Riley. Do you have to be home?"

Riley turned to look at her mom, who shook her head and gestured toward the door.

"No." Riley felt like she was seeing Lucas—the real Lucas—again for the first time in forever. "We could go somewhere and talk."

"I'd like that."

"Yeah, like you used to when it was easy," Mrs. Matthews said, giving them a little nudge out the door and closing it before turning back to glare at her husband. "'Let the kids live,' huh? 'Let the kids live,' huh? Hah!" As she stormed toward the kitchen, she really started shouting. "Dewey! Get back here! We're not done, *Dewey*. . . ."

As Mr. Matthews watched his wife stomp

toward their son's room, panic flashed across his face. "*Run*, Doy!" he shouted.

But Mrs. Matthews was determined. She wasn't going to let that little boy turn to dust. She was going to exert just the right kind of pressure and turn him into a child who not only could say his name correctly but would sparkle and shine like a diamond, bright as the morning dew.

CHAPTER 8

Riley and Lucas were back at Topanga's in the same matching orange chairs. But this time they had their own smoothies—and they were looking directly at each other.

"All right, so the pressure's off. We're friends now," Lucas said. "What do you want to talk about?"

Even though they'd broken up, Riley felt like they were in a different kind of friend zone than before, so she was still a bit tentative. "What do you talk about when you're with your friends?"

"Well, when I'm with my friends, we usually talk about sports," Lucas replied. "Do you know anything about sports?"

Riley shook her head. She wasn't supposed to talk about sports with her *ex-boyfriend*, was she? He could do that with his guy friends, but not with her. Right?

"No?" Lucas didn't seem to believe her. "Any sports? What about basketball? You know anything about basketball?"

"Yeah," Riley admitted carefully.

"Yeah?" Lucas's blue eyes sparkled with excitement.

"Yeah, yeah." Riley nodded. She didn't want to give away too much.

"Yeah? Maybe?" Lucas was apparently determined to drag it out of her.

All right, fine. She released the pressure she was putting on herself before it, too, turned them to dust. "Well, we're in New York, so obviously my favorite team is the Knicks," she began before picking up speed and really laying it all out there in a stream-of-consciousness flurry. "And you know, this may not be our best year, but at the end of the day it doesn't matter, because we have Melo and we have Phil Jackson and that's all that counts. We shouldn't have traded J. R. Smith! But at the end of the day, you know what? It's not our best season and we have a terrible record and we're the *worst* in the NBA. I am at Madison Square Garden and I see all these fake fans just jumping onto bandwagons like the Heat or something like that and you know what? That is not what a true fan is! If you're gonna be at the Garden, you better represent the Knicks!"

The longer Riley went on, the more surprised Lucas appeared, until she finally wrapped it up and coyly added, "But yeah, I don't really know that much, obviously."

"I really like you, Riley," Lucas said softly, again.

Riley giggled in spite of herself. Maybe they weren't boyfriend and girlfriend anymore. But even without a label to define them, there was still *something* between them: a little bit more than friends, a little bit less than a couple—and that was more than fine with Riley.

At school the next day, Riley and Lucas walked in together. But they weren't about to let anybody pressure them into making a bigger deal out of that than it was.

"Hey!" Riley shouted when they got to the top of the steps overlooking the indoor quad. "Lucas and I are friends. That's what we are. That's what we've always been. And we're not going to hurt that because you guys want us to be something we're not. So go back to your own lives, because nobody is moving too fast here."

As Lucas and Riley smiled at each other, confident and firm in their decision, Farkle and Maya appeared in the quad—Maya in a lacy white wedding dress and Farkle in a black tuxedo and top hat.

"'Sup?" Maya shouted to Riley as she and Farkle headed for history class. On their way, Maya tossed a bouquet directly at Riley, who caught it.

Lucas looked into Riley's eyes. She looked back into his. Then, with a quick laugh, she handed the bouquet over to Darby and Yogi, and she and Lucas